What it was like in ...

ANCIENT BENIN

DAVID LONG

Illustrated by
Stefano Tambellini

Barrington Stoke

For the children and staff of Boxford School

Published by Barrington Stoke
An imprint of HarperCollins*Publishers*
1 Robroyston Gate, Glasgow, G33 1JN

www.barringtonstoke.co.uk

HarperCollins*Publishers*
Macken House, 39/40 Mayor Street Upper,
Dublin 1, DO1 C9W8, Ireland

First published in 2026

Text © 2026 David Long
Illustrations © 2026 Stefano Tambellini
Cover design © 2026 HarperCollins*Publishers* Limited

The moral right of David Long and Stefano Tambellini to be identified as the author and illustrator of this work has been asserted in accordance with the Copyright, Designs and Patents Act, 1988

ISBN 978-0-00-874599-8

10 9 8 7 6 5 4 3 2 1

All rights reserved. No part of this publication may be reproduced, stored in a retrieval system, or transmitted, in whole or in any part in any form or by any means, electronic, mechanical, photocopying, recording or otherwise without the prior permission in writing of the publisher and copyright owners

Without limiting the exclusive rights of any author, contributor or the publisher of this publication, any unauthorised use of this publication to train generative artificial intelligence (AI) technologies is expressly prohibited. HarperCollins also exercise their rights under Article 4(3) of the Digital Single Market Directive 2019/790 and expressly reserve this publication from the text and data mining exception

The contents of this publication are believed correct at the time of printing. Nevertheless the publisher can accept no responsibility for errors or omissions, changes in the detail given or for any expense or loss thereby caused

A catalogue record for this book is available from the British Library

Printed and bound in India by Replika Press Pvt. Ltd.

CONTENTS

1 THE FOREST KINGDOM — 1
Who Were the Ancient Edo?

2 WARRIOR-KINGS AND WALLS — 9
Rulers and the People They Ruled

3 MAKERS AND TRADERS — 23
Daily Life in Benin City

4 FAMILIES OF THE FOREST — 35
Farming, Foraging and Finding Leopards

5 FESTIVALS AND FUN — 46
Religion, Gods and Games

6 THE SLAVE COAST — 57
Selling Palm Oil, Pepper and People

7 THE BENIN BRONZES — 67
A Library Made of Metal

8 THE SCRAMBLE FOR AFRICA — 75
How Did the Kingdom End?

9 LIFE IN NIGERIA — 86
The Edo People Today

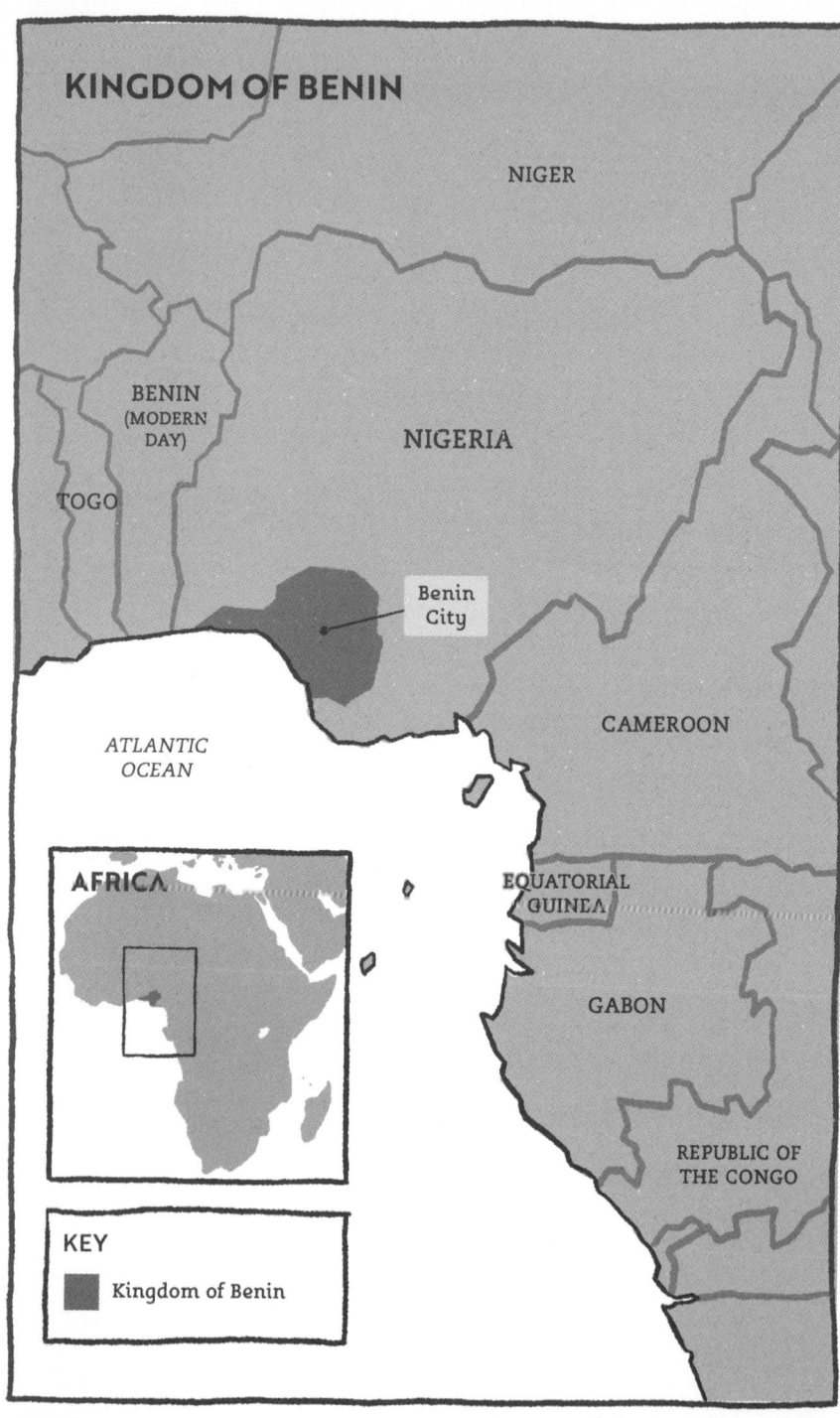

1
THE FOREST KINGDOM

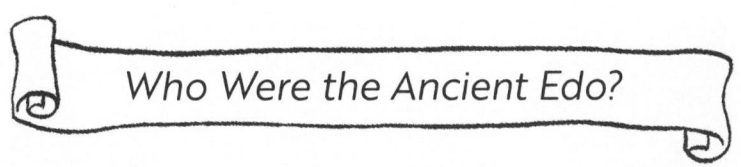

Who Were the Ancient Edo?

The ancient Edo people lived in the Kingdom of Benin, a country on the west coast of Africa. The Kingdom of Benin was small but rich and powerful. It lasted for more than 700 years but disappeared in the nineteenth century when the land became part of Nigeria. This means the country described in this book is not the same as the modern one called Benin, which is further along the African coast.

A thousand years ago, this part of Africa was mostly hidden away in the dense

THE FOREST KINGDOM

rainforest. It was known as Igodomigodo, and its rulers were called the Ogisos.

The people living in the forest at that time believed that their rulers were part king and part god, but we don't know very much about the Ogisos because nothing was written down about them.

THE FOREST KINGDOM

The details we do know come from the myths and legends that the Edo people used to tell each other. These stories were an important way of passing information down from one generation to the next, and the best storytellers were known as *griots*.

In the twelfth century, the Edo decided that they no longer wanted to be ruled by the Ogisos, and they were made to leave the kingdom. We don't exactly know why this happened or what went wrong, but the chiefs of the forest people chose a new leader instead. Ogiso meant "ruler of the sky", but the new leader was called the Oba, which is another word for "king".

The first Oba was Eweka. He soon had complete power over every man, woman and child in the kingdom. All the land belonged to Eweka, and he was in charge of the army. He also controlled the buying and selling of goods between the Edo and all the neighbouring tribes.

THE FOREST KINGDOM

Eweka became very rich as a result of this, and he went on to rule the kingdom for 35 years.

For a long time, most Edo families lived in villages and small settlements in clearings. There, they were surrounded by the trees and thick greenery of the rainforest. They worked as farmers and hunters, catching and killing things to eat.

Living in groups meant the Edo were able to defend themselves against attack from other tribes in the region. It may also have given them protection from the dangerous animals they lived alongside in the forest. These included man-eating lions and leopards, crocodiles, poisonous snakes and ferocious wild pigs.

As the villages grew in size, some of the larger ones began to take over other smaller settlements. These grew to become towns, and several of them came together to form a big city. This was first named Edo, then later Benin City, and it was the most important place in the kingdom.

The Oba lived in the centre of the city in a vast and luxurious palace. The palace was so large that it may have covered a third of the entire city. Behind its walls and towers, the Oba had hundreds of servants to look after him and his family. There were also chiefs

THE FOREST KINGDOM

and senior army officers and advisers who helped the Oba to run the country.

Over many years, the kingdom expanded until it was one of the richest and most advanced empires in this part of Africa. This happened because the Oba's army was large and very well trained, and the soldiers had much better weapons than any of their rivals. This meant Edo troops were able to conquer more and more land, enslaving the men and women who lived there.

The Kingdom of Benin's success continued when the Edo met Europeans for the first time. First came sailors, who arrived on ships from Portugal towards the end of the fifteenth century. The ships were called caravels, and the sailors were excited to see this strange, new land.

In particular, they were impressed by the enormous size of the capital city. Everything in it seemed much finer than anything else along the African coast: its wide straight roads, the Oba's huge palace and the other grand buildings.

The Portuguese sailors were keen to trade with the Oba and his people. They wanted to fill their ships with unusual goods from Africa that they could sell for large sums of money when they got back home. The sailors

THE FOREST KINGDOM

began buying sacks of exotic spices, gold and elephant ivory. They paid for them with guns and other things that the Edo people couldn't find in Africa or make themselves.

Other traders began to arrive too – from Holland, France, Spain and England. They all wanted more and more goods from the Edo. For a while, this made the Oba even richer, but he refused to share his wealth with his people, and many ordinary Edo felt that this was unfair.

Increased trade also caused arguments between the Oba and the Europeans. Eventually this led to a violent tragedy, which you can read about later in this book. The violence led to the sudden end of the Kingdom of Benin.

2
WARRIOR-KINGS AND WALLS

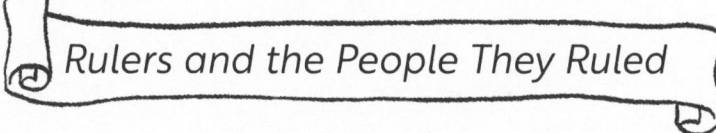
Rulers and the People They Ruled

The early European travellers were very impressed by the network of high walls that the Edo had created to protect Benin City and their Oba's palace.

The massive walls were built using hundreds of thousands of tonnes of dried mud, but sadly almost nothing of them has survived for us to see today.

Because so little of it exists, historians still argue about the true size of the walled area.

We do know that the walls themselves were tall, strong and extremely long. Some visitors thought they might have been as high as 20 metres in parts, and that they stretched for an incredible 16,000 kilometres. That's about the distance between Australia and England.

This figure probably isn't accurate, but Benin City must still have been one of the largest building sites anywhere in the ancient world.

These gigantic defences would have taken many years to complete. Several Europeans reported that many of the finished walls were beautifully decorated. They completely surrounded the Oba's palace and also protected large houses lining the city's main roads. It's likely that armed soldiers stood guard at each gateway into the city.

The walls were necessary because the Kingdom of Benin wasn't a peaceful place to

WARRIOR-KINGS AND WALLS

live. Many of the Obas were warrior-kings – fierce rulers who would order thousands of their soldiers to attack other tribes in the region. One Oba, Ozolua, was so good at this that it is believed he won more than 200 battles.

Another amazing thing about the city was that its streets were brightly lit at night-time. This was very unusual 500 years ago. The light

was produced by burning oil from palm trees in lamps. The hundreds of glowing lamps must have made the area around the palace look even more spectacular after dark than it did during the day.

However, the Oba rarely left his palace to travel along its streets or to see what had been built. This meant the two million people he ruled hardly ever got to see him, not even from a distance. Those who did meet the Oba had to get down on their knees as a sign of respect. He was treated almost like a god, and no one was allowed to look directly at his face without permission.

Most Edo probably had no idea of what their ruler looked like. This must have made him seem even more powerful because he was so mysterious to them. In fact, many Edo started believing the Oba could survive without eating or sleeping and that he never needed to wash himself!

Only men could become an Oba and rule the Kingdom of Benin, but royal women were also highly respected by visitors to the palace. Some of them played an important part in ruling the kingdom alongside the Oba. One of the most famous was Ozolua's wife, who was called Idia.

We know that after the death of Ozolua in 1504, their son Esigie became the next Oba and Idia had a lot of power. She may even have helped defeat the Igala tribesmen who had always been an enemy of the Edo and sometimes tried to steal some of their land.

Idia was the Iyoba, meaning the mother of the Oba, and was given her own palace. This was on the edge of the city, and she had her own servants and advisers. The palace may have been given to Idia as a reward because the wife of an Oba had never survived after his death before.

Prior to Idia, an Oba's wife would be murdered as soon as the new Oba took over the throne. Idia somehow managed to avoid this happening to her.

Another tradition was that only the Oba and his most senior chiefs and army officers could wear beads made of red coral. However, there is a beautiful ivory mask of Idia on display in a museum in Germany that has some coral beads on it. This shows that she had been given permission to wear them.

The mask proves just how special Idia was. Red was the most important colour in the Kingdom of Benin, and coral was a very rare and valuable luxury.

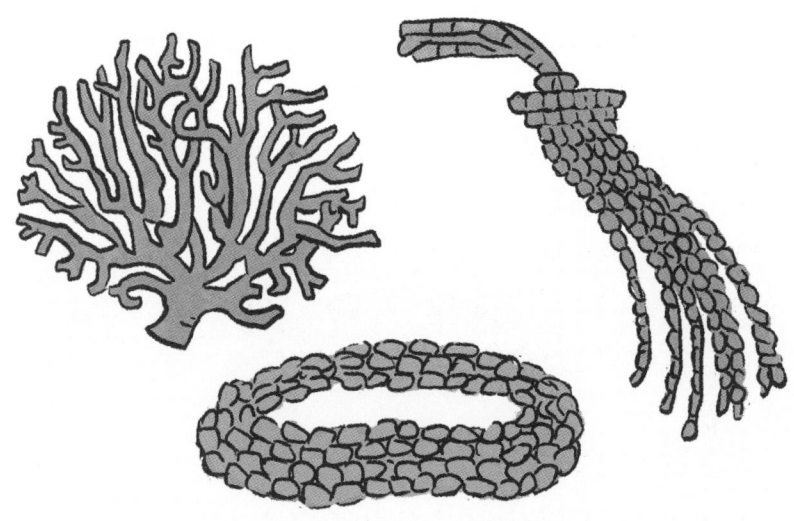

It mostly came from the Mediterranean Sea, which meant it had to be carried hundreds of miles across the scorching hot Sahara Desert. This was a very difficult and dangerous journey done on foot or by camel, which made the coral even more precious and expensive.

The Edo believed that red stones such as coral, agate and jasper had magical powers – a sort of supernatural energy which they called *ase*.

The Oba often dressed entirely in red to show how rich and important he was. His clothes included an amazing long red tunic woven from strings of polished coral beads. The power of these beads was thought to grow even stronger if the coral was washed every year in cow's blood.

Because of this, only special palace staff called *enisen* were allowed to handle the beads and fine ivory that made the Oba look so magnificent.

Ordinary people enjoyed none of these luxuries, of course. The kingdom may have grown rich by conquering land and trading goods, but the wealth wasn't shared among everyone living there. In fact, the Obas were richer than everyone else put together, so the clothes most men and women wore were simple and very basic.

Instead of expensive beads of coral, their clothing was made from plant fibres woven into a rough cloth. People wrapped these around their bodies like sheets. They certainly weren't designed to impress anyone or to look fashionable and stylish.

OBA

ORDINARY MAN

Some people made a living by carving coral and ivory with incredible skill, yet they could not afford to wear any of the rings, bracelets and other items of jewellery that they created. These rare and wonderful things were all reserved for the Obas and their families, plus a few of the most important people around them.

3
MAKERS AND TRADERS

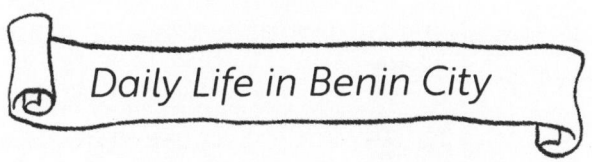
Daily Life in Benin City

Hundreds of Edo people were employed to create beautiful, costly objects for the Oba and his palace. These workers were members of groups called craft guilds, and they were mostly men. The guilds were official organisations in which people with the same skills worked together designing and creating similar things in an area of the city.

In the same way that the enisen were responsible for the most important royal items made of coral and ivory worn by the king, other guild members performed

MAKERS AND TRADERS

different duties that ordinary people were not allowed to do.

For example, if the Oba wanted a new *eben* (a type of ceremonial sword), a member of the Guild of Blacksmiths would make one for him. If the Oba became ill, palace servants would order the Guild of Doctors to send someone to provide advice and medicines. Each guild was responsible for a different task. Their members included the kingdom's most

Craft Guilds

talented metalworkers and leatherworkers, as well as weavers, potters, dancers, drummers and even acrobats.

These guilds were very important to the Oba. They were a way of making sure that the people working for him were properly trained and the very best at what they did. Children usually followed their parents into the same guild workshops, and so the skills and expertise needed to make a sword or

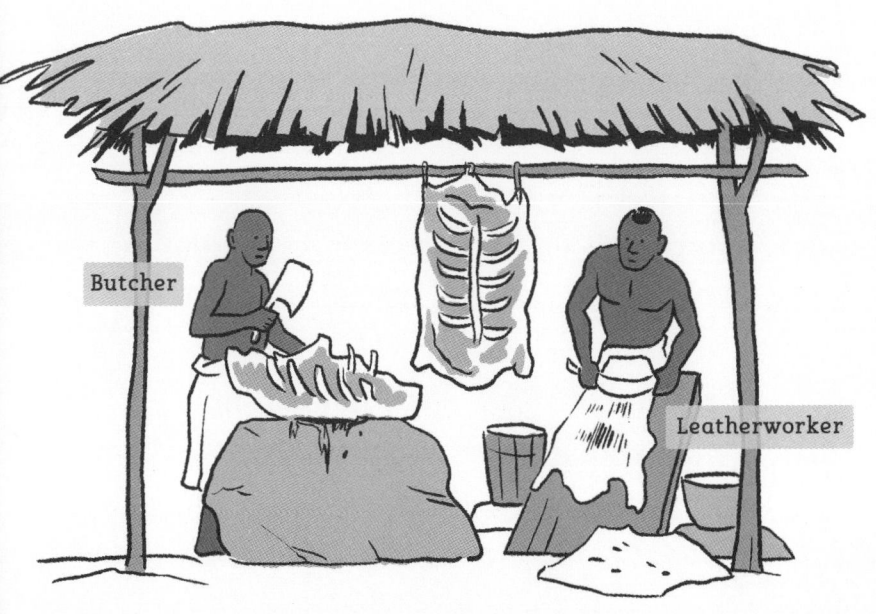

a mask or a drum were shared and passed down from one generation to the next.

Historians think there were more than 60 different guilds altogether. Many of them existed for hundreds of years. A few may even have served the Ogisos before the first Oba came to the throne.

Not everyone in Benin worked for the Oba or was in a craft guild, however. Many workers made more basic items, and they may have worked alone. These were the kind of objects ordinary families used every day, such as cooking pots and tools. The people who made them were less skilled than the members of the guilds, but the things they made were just as important for the families who lived in and around Benin City.

All this meant that the Kingdom of Benin was a divided society, like most early civilisations. There were enormous differences between the daily lives of rich families and poor ones.

Males and females also had different roles in the Kingdom of Benin. Edo children didn't go to school or learn the sorts of things children do today. Instead, boys were taught work skills by their fathers and older brothers. Girls learned to make clothes and were shown how to prepare and cook food by their mothers and sisters.

These lessons were important because young children were expected to work like adults from the age of six or seven.

Mostly, this meant staying at home if you were a girl or going out to work in the fields or a workshop if you were a boy.

MAKERS AND TRADERS

Large numbers of Edo must have been employed as builders too, constructing the walls around Benin City and maintaining them when they were finished.

There were certain jobs that women simply weren't allowed to do, such as be in the army. Most of them were expected to get married, have children and look after the house. Some also made and decorated pots at home or wove colourful striped cloth to turn into clothes.

MAKERS AND TRADERS

Women could make a living buying and selling these things at their local markets. The striped cloth was particularly popular, and women who were good at trading may have become fairly rich merchants.

At the Market

Socialising

Pots

Bartering

MAKERS AND TRADERS

Local markets were vital in Benin and other West African countries because there were no shops, bars or restaurants. Stalls offered all sorts of items for sale – everything from live farm animals to household goods, clothing and food.

But people didn't just go to markets to buy and sell. The market was also an important meeting place, and people often went there to exchange gossip and hear the latest news.

For hundreds of years, the Edo didn't have coins or paper money to shop with like we do today. They mostly got goods by bartering with each other.

Barter is an ancient system where the buyer and seller agree to swap one kind of item for another. This meant prices for things went up and down all the time depending on how rare an item was and how badly the buyer wanted it. This sounds confusing, but bartering worked well for thousands of years and has been used all over the world.

*

Many people who worked for the Oba inherited their jobs, meaning that when a government official or a servant got ill or died, their job would be taken over by one of their children. But sometimes jobs went to individuals who had a particular skill or to people the Oba wished to reward because members of their families had done something brave or remarkable.

The army was another large employer of fit young men and boys. For a while, the Kingdom of Benin's army was one of the largest in this part of Africa, and at times it might have included around 20,000 troops.

Unfortunately, not much is known about the Edos' fighting methods, or the lives of any individual soldiers. Even so, we can tell from the Oba's success in conquering other lands that it must have been a very effective fighting force. This was especially true during the reign of an Oba called Ewuare the Great in the middle of the fifteenth century.

Of course, fighting in battle was one of the most dangerous jobs to have in Benin. Thousands of soldiers must have died even when their army won.

4

FAMILIES OF THE FOREST

Farming, Foraging and Finding Leopards

Most Edo families eventually moved into Benin City, but some stayed behind in the rainforest. They carried on living much like their ancestors had done centuries before in the days of the Ogisos.

These people had very different lives to those in the city. They built small huts for themselves out of mud and branches, with roofs made from palm leaves.

FAMILIES OF THE FOREST

A typical family hut was small and basic, with just one room for everyone. Some rural communities in Africa still live like this today, and villagers still clear patches of land outside their huts so they and their children can grow fruit and vegetables to eat.

The forests of Africa were dangerous places for humans, full of ferocious wild animals and poisonous plants, as well as many evil spirits who hid in the shadows, according to Edo legends. But they were also a rich source of things that the villagers needed to survive.

The materials they used to build their huts were gathered from the forest. Firewood was collected for cooking, and they gathered fresh ingredients such as berries to add to the crops they grew themselves.

The forest dwellers must have enjoyed a varied and healthy diet that changed from season to season according to the weather.

Some of the most important plants they grew were things we still eat today, such as rice, beans, okra and brightly coloured peppers. Yams and plantains were very popular too, as these could be cooked on a fire and eaten hot or cold.

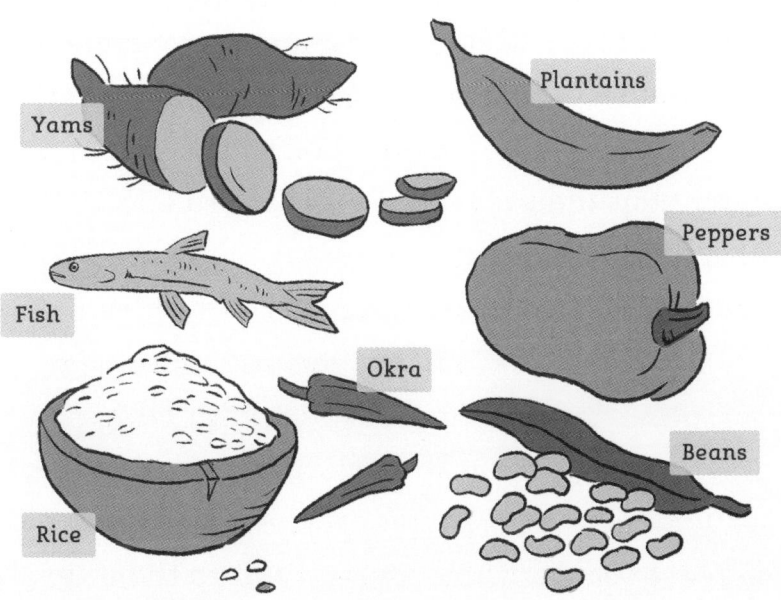

Meat stews and roast fish were delicious treats but saved for special occasions even in families that raised their own sheep, cattle, goats and chickens. The Edo also caught and killed wild birds and other species whenever they could. Families living near a river or the sea would catch tasty shellfish. The Edo also harvested plants to make into medicines.

The main meal was probably served in the evening, when everyone had returned to their huts after a long, hard working day. If any of the families managed to grow, gather or catch more than they could eat themselves, the extra could be sold at the local market or traded with other villagers.

Even living deep in the forest, village life was never lonely. Families met with each other all the time. Most villages and small settlements had a central place where groups of people could sit in the evenings to listen to a griot telling stories.

Storytelling was an important part of Edo life in both the city and the forest. Spoken stories were a way of remembering people and events, and passing them on to children. Historians call this oral history, and when there are no written records, it is often the only way for us today to understand what really happened in the past.

Some of the stories were a bit like the fairy tales we know today. Stories the Edos liked listening to could be funny or scary or maybe even both at the same time.

Often the stories were meant to teach people important lessons – such as don't go into the forest after dark or you'll get into trouble.

A story like this might sound like it's about an imaginary man or woman who ignores the warnings and is never seen again because they met an evil spirit in the forest. However, there was a very real risk of a person getting lost in the woods and then being eaten alive by a lion or crocodile.

FAMILIES OF THE FOREST

Despite this danger, we know that some of the Edo went into the rainforest looking for trouble. These were the young hunters who had one of the most exciting and most dangerous jobs in the whole of the kingdom. It was their job to find and catch Benin's famous forest leopards.

The leopards were probably the most impressive animals many of the Edo ever saw. They were thought of as the "kings of the forest", and the Edo admired them for their hunting skills, their beauty and their sharp claws and teeth. The leopards became an important symbol of the wealth and power of the Obas.

Many of the rulers kept leopards as pets to remind people of this. Leopard sculptures made of ivory or bronze were used to decorate some of the great halls in the palace. Some sculptures showed an Oba holding a couple of ferocious leopards by their tails, probably

FAMILIES OF THE FOREST

as a way of demonstrating how brave and strong he was.

Today, even King Charles III has a pair of ancient ivory leopards from Benin. These were presented to Queen Victoria (his great-great-great-grandmother), and each one took five whole elephant tusks to make. This would be illegal today because elephants have become endangered as a result of people killing them for their ivory.

Back in the rainforest, the young men who belonged to the Guild of Leopard Hunters were believed to have special magical powers that protected them from danger. In fact, they risked injury and even death every time they went out hunting for the best animals to bring back to the palace.

Some of the leopards the men caught spent the rest of their lives in captivity at the palace. This meant ordinary people only saw them on the rare occasions that the Oba was seen in public.

Sadly, many leopards were killed for their valuable skins and teeth. These may have been used to decorate the royal throne or presented to successful military commanders, like medals given out today. Leopard skins were also sold to European traders, who were happy to pay a very high price for anything from such a rare and exotic creature.

5
FESTIVALS AND FUN

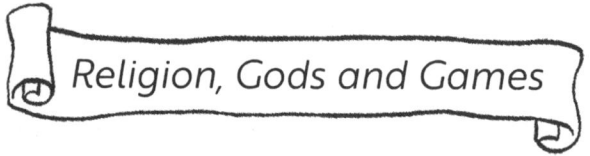

Religion, Gods and Games

Religion was an important part of life for everyone in Benin, but it was very complicated. The Edo were polytheistic, which means they worshipped many different gods instead of just one god, like Christians, Muslims and Jews do.

The Edo also believed there were two different worlds – the real one in which they lived and a spirit one. These were connected, but in ways that are not easy to understand.

The gods the Edo worshipped were the children of Osanobua, the chief god who they believed created the world. The Obas also claimed that they were descendants of Osanobua.

The Edo thought that different gods affected their lives in different ways. They believed gods could help a man and wife have lots of healthy children, make a family's crops grow tall and strong, or simply end a person's life. Some wild animals, including crocodiles and snakes, were associated with the gods and thought to have magical spirits.

Olokun was Osanobua's eldest son, and he was believed to control the oceans and the rivers. Ogun was the god of iron, so he was very important to soldiers, farmers and hunters who used weapons and tools made of this metal. Osun was a forest god and the god of medicine, magic and healing. He was responsible for the plants that the Edo picked and used to cure sickness.

The god of death was Ogiuwu, who had a helper called Ofoe. Ofoe was thought to have no body, just legs for chasing people and arms for catching them. Once Ofoe had caught someone and taken them back to Ogiuwu, they couldn't escape. That person's life was over, and he or she vanished into the spirit world.

Not everyone worshipped the same gods at the same time, so there were many different ceremonies held during the year.

FESTIVALS AND FUN

Some of these were small and personal, such as a warrior quietly praying to Ogun before going into battle.

Other ceremonies were gruesome and bloodthirsty, and the worst involved human sacrifices. These meant murdering large numbers of innocent people as a way of showing the community's love and respect for a particular god.

Some religious festivals were very large and lively and colourful, involving hundreds of people at a time.

For example, when the yams were ready to eat, festivals were held over several days to honour Osun and Ogun. Everyone hoped they would give the farmers a good harvest so they could all eat well for the rest of the year.

Sometimes even the Oba joined in by using an *egogo* to keep the evil spirits away from his people. An egogo was a type of bell made of bronze or carved ivory.

This was one of the rare occasions that the Oba left his palace. When this happened, people would stop working and walk into the centre of Benin City hoping to see their king and his pet leopards.

FESTIVALS AND FUN

The Oba would bless his people like a priest, but only after making sure that he looked as impressive as he could.

He used fine clothes, expensive corals and ivory jewels to remind everyone else of the link between himself, his royal ancestors and the Edo gods.

Festivals could be fun as well as serious, but the Edo had many other ways of enjoying themselves when they weren't farming or fighting wars. Music was important throughout West Africa, particularly music that used percussion instruments such as bells, drums, clappers and gourds. A gourd is a dry, hard-skinned fruit that makes a hollow sound when it is hit with a stick.

FESTIVALS AND FUN

Instruments like these were played by women as well as men, and the noise they made could be very loud. Playing loudly was believed to attract the gods' attention, especially when trained dancers began moving to the rhythm of many different instruments.

Sports and games were also popular in the kingdom, and the Edo are thought to have enjoyed many of the activities that are still common across West Africa today.

Wrestling and boxing matches were useful ways for young men to keep fit, as well as giving them a chance to show off their strength and skill. One form of boxing, now known as *dambe*, involved fighters kicking their opponents as well as punching them. Each man had one of his fists wrapped in cloth or rope. He used this to hit his opponent as hard as possible and his other arm as a shield to avoid getting hurt himself.

Happily, there is no evidence that small children joined in with this sort of thing, but we do know some of the games that young Edo played hundreds of years ago. One game is called *oware*, and people still play it, making it one of the oldest games in the world.

Oware is a game of strategy, often using small pebbles or plant seeds as playing pieces, and the aim is to capture more pieces than

FESTIVALS AND FUN 55

your opponent. Today, people play with oware boards that have pits or cups to hold the pieces, while originally people probably dropped the pieces into holes scooped out of the ground.

Another game was a bit like tag. The children all stood in a circle except one who was outside it holding an object. This could be anything that could fit in one hand. The player walked round the circle and placed the object on the ground behind one of the other players without them noticing. Then they ran the whole way round the circle at top speed, trying not to be caught by the person they'd placed the object behind. If they got round, they took the other player's place in the circle, and it became the chaser's turn to drop the object behind someone else. It sounds a tiring but exciting game and could be fun to try out with some friends!

6
THE SLAVE COAST

Selling Palm Oil, Pepper and People

The Edo were very successful traders, but there was a dark and horrible side to this activity.

The Portuguese visitors who arrived in the fifteenth century were friendly at first and mostly interested in buying simple things like peppercorns and palm oil.

Pepper was cheap in Benin, but back in Portugal it was expensive. Like other spices, it was used by cooks to flavour meals and to disguise the taste when ingredients were beginning to go off. This happened all the time before the invention of the refrigerator, especially with meat and fish. Palm oil was also used in cooking, as well as in lamps, soap and even medicines.

The Obas controlled all the trade with people living outside their kingdom. At first this meant only trading with neighbouring tribes, but it came to include the Portuguese and other Europeans.

The Obas were naturally pleased to have this chance to increase their wealth further. They exchanged goods made or grown in their own country for things the Europeans offered, such as guns and alcohol.

Some luxury items were traded in this way too, including carved ivories, colourful cotton cloth and leopard skins. The demand for these grew fast as many more Europeans set sail for West Africa. The Obas could get

THE SLAVE COAST

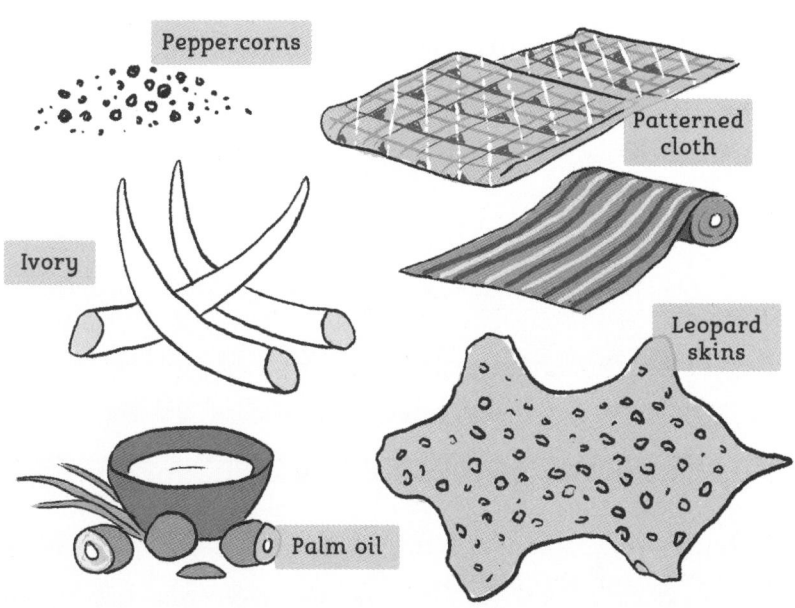

whatever they wanted to sell from their people cheaply and easily, and trade it profitably with the Europeans.

It wasn't long before Portugal became the first country to buy humans from the Kingdom of Benin and send them thousands of miles across the Atlantic Ocean.

Many people died on these long voyages because conditions on board the ships were horrific. The bodies of the sick and dead were just thrown overboard, and survivors were forced to work on land the Portuguese had conquered in what is now Brazil.

The Spanish, Dutch and English quickly followed the Portuguese and began buying

people too and sending these enslaved people to their colonies overseas. Before long, trading human lives had become such an important export for West African rulers like the Obas that this part of Africa became known as the Slave Coast.

While this is shocking, the Portuguese did not invent slavery. The Obas didn't either, although Benin was very involved in it. The enslavement of people had existed in almost every ancient civilisation going back thousands of years, but of course it is still a deeply upsetting subject. While rich European countries weren't the first to buy and sell African men and women in this way, they were responsible for the rapid expansion of the trade of enslaved people because they wanted to send them to their colonies.

Historians aren't sure exactly how this trade worked in the Kingdom of Benin. However, most of them agree that the Obas and their senior chieftains were personally involved. We also know that Benin's rulers made themselves much, much richer from the misery and murder they inflicted on their fellow Africans.

We know this because Europeans visiting the Kingdom of Benin were strictly forbidden to travel inland from the coast. The few who decided to go against this and explore the country anyway died of strange tropical diseases, and this terrified the others. Most

THE SLAVE COAST

Europeans became too scared to risk leaving their ships, so they can't have raided the kingdom themselves or captured the people who were enslaved and transported across the Atlantic.

Instead, it was the Edo themselves who were catching and selling many people every year. The enslaved people included men, women and even children taken prisoner after battles with rival tribes, but some may have been other Edo people.

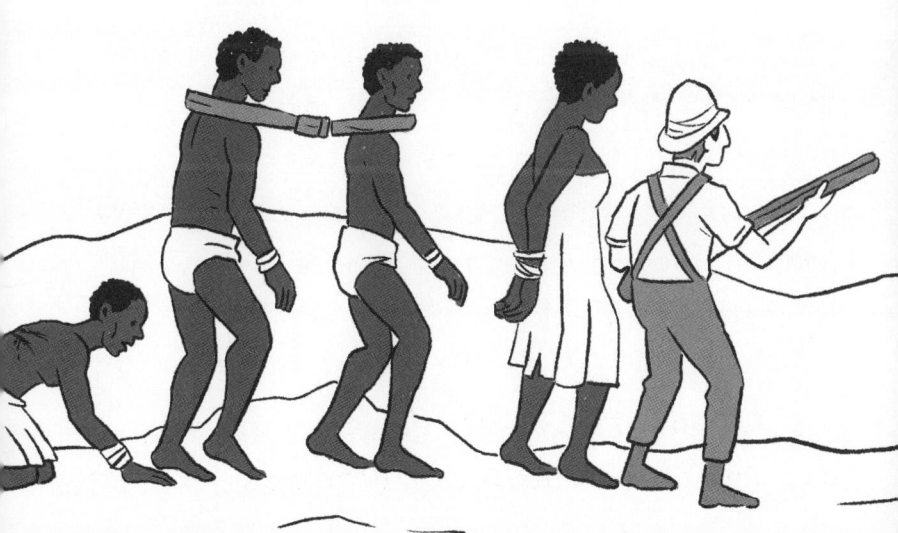

A few of the victims probably became the property of the Oba and ended up working for him.

Many more were sold to European and American buyers and faced a lifetime of enslavement. The trade was so profitable that it continued this way for hundreds of years.

Countries like the Kingdom of Benin and nearby Dahomey were reluctant to stop it, no matter how cruel the trade was and how unpopular it made them across Africa.

Money from enslaving people gave a ruler the ability to equip more of his soldiers with guns. Superior weapons made the army stronger, and this meant the Oba could invade even more land and capture more prisoners to enslave and sell.

Millions of lives were ruined in this way and countless communities destroyed for ever. Benin's involvement in enslaving people was also a factor in the kingdom's eventual collapse many decades later.

A warrior and his attendants

The head of an Oba

A horn player

Two acrobats in a ceremony

A cow being sacrificed

An Oba on a horse

7

THE BENIN BRONZES

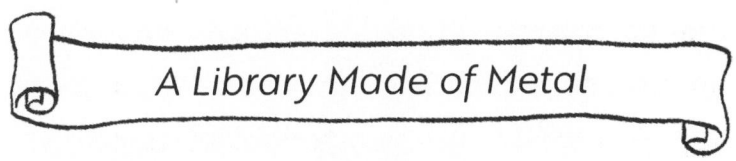

A Library Made of Metal

The Benin Bronzes are a large and impressive collection of mostly metal objects created by Edo craftsmen from around the sixteenth century onwards. These were mainly made for the Oba's palace, and it is likely that at various times, thousands of different bronze sculptures and plaques were displayed within its walls.

Despite its name, not all the pieces in the collection are bronze, which is a mixture of two metals: copper and tin. Some are brass, which is copper mixed with zinc, while others are made from materials such as wood, ivory, leather and bone. The collection shows the objects were made by some exceptionally talented craftsmen, much like the other beautiful pieces the Edo produced using ivory, coral or wood.

A lot of the workmanship is so good that some Europeans refused to believe that the bronzes could have been made in Africa. In the past, many white people looked down on other races, and so they assumed the bronzes must have come from a different country, not a place most people had never even heard of.

The amazing quality of the craftsmanship helps explain why a single small bronze was sold in 2015 for an incredible £10 million. Some historians say the real value is even higher than this because the bronzes tell us so much about life in Benin City hundreds of years ago. Many of the items are so detailed that the collection has been described as a library of metal – a source of secret stories and exciting clues about the past.

THE BENIN BRONZES

We know the Edo began making fine metal objects about a thousand years ago despite metal being very hard to find in their country then. Many more artists worked with metal from the 1500s, which was when European ships began arriving with fresh supplies of metal that their captains were happy to trade.

These ships carried other unusual items to Benin, including wooden chests full of cowries and brass manillas.

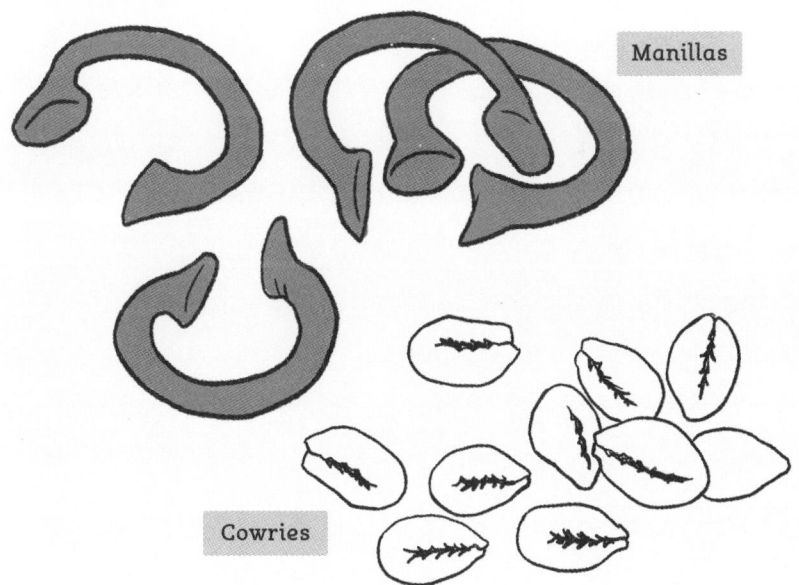

Manillas

Cowries

Cowries are beautiful seashells that people in this part of Africa started using as a form of money.

Manillas are heavy, horseshoe-shaped bracelets that were also used this way; however, they were often melted down by Edo craftsmen who needed the metal to make more bronze items.

How to make a bronze leopard statue

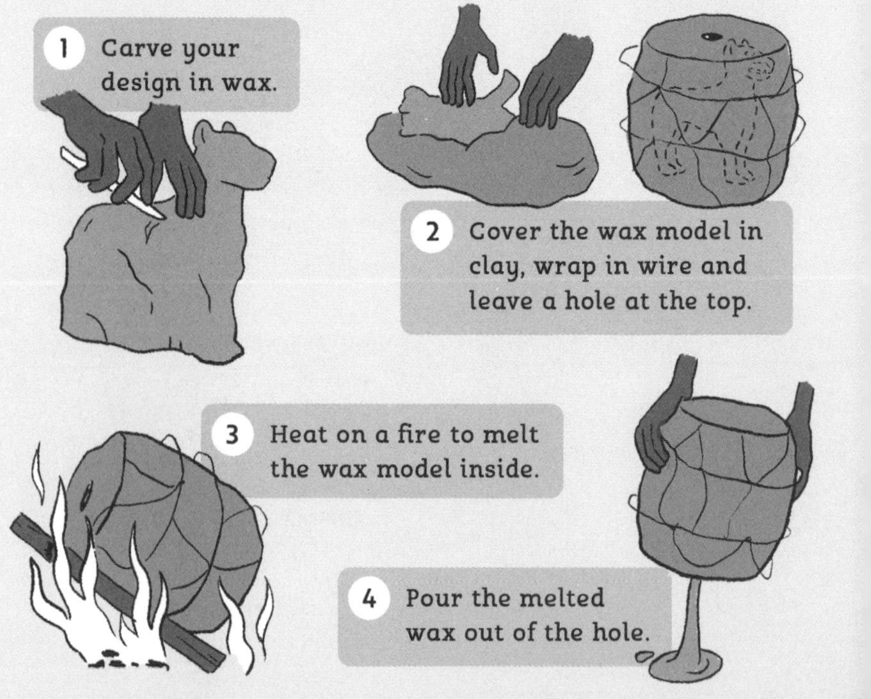

1. Carve your design in wax.
2. Cover the wax model in clay, wrap in wire and leave a hole at the top.
3. Heat on a fire to melt the wax model inside.
4. Pour the melted wax out of the hole.

The pieces they created tell us a lot about life in the Kingdom of Benin, yet some important information is missing. For example, none of the bronzes include scenes of everyday life. There are no sculptures of farmers planting crops in their fields or children playing games. None of the items show artists or craftsmen hard at work or mothers weaving or cooking for their families.

5. Pour melted bronze into the mould and cool.
6. Break the clay off.
7. File and polish to make it shine.
8. The finished design!

In fact, there are very few women at all in the bronzes, which is extraordinary as they made up at least half of the population. It means the collection tells an incomplete story about life in this lost civilisation, but it is still a fascinating one.

Many of the bronzes include scenes from inside the royal palace. Others show events such as military victories, royal processions and the activities of the Oba and his senior officials.

There are even a few statues of Portuguese soldiers and sailors. These give us an idea of how strange Europeans must have looked to the Edo, with their thin faces, long noses and pointy beards. They also show the importance of international trade in the long history of the kingdom.

The bronzes that show Obas are interesting in different ways. They were clearly intended to impress visitors to the palace by demonstrating the king's wealth and power, much like his red coral clothes and pet leopards.

Showing an Oba with a crocodile or a giant python was a way of reminding everyone that he was related to Olokun, the great god of the oceans and rivers.

In other bronzes, the Oba has legs made of mudfish, a rare African species that can survive out of the water as well as in it. It may seem strange to portray the Oba with legs shaped like a fish, but for the Edo it was a way of saying that their ruler was master of the sea as well as the land.

Unusual details like these mean the Benin Bronzes are very interesting to look at, but they were clearly even more important to the people who created them. In fact, we now know that the bronzes weren't just beautifully crafted objects made to please the Oba. For their makers, they were extraordinary and unique expressions of Edo culture, tradition and community.

8
THE SCRAMBLE FOR AFRICA

How Did the Kingdom End?

Strong nations have always invaded weaker ones so they can dominate the inhabitants by taxing them and stealing their land. Some of the most warlike countries became mighty empires this way while making their rulers even richer and more powerful.

Soon after the first Europeans began arriving in Benin, soldiers from Spain and Portugal conquered large parts of Central and South America. The Spanish had crossed the Atlantic Ocean hoping to discover El Dorado – according to legend, this was the world's most

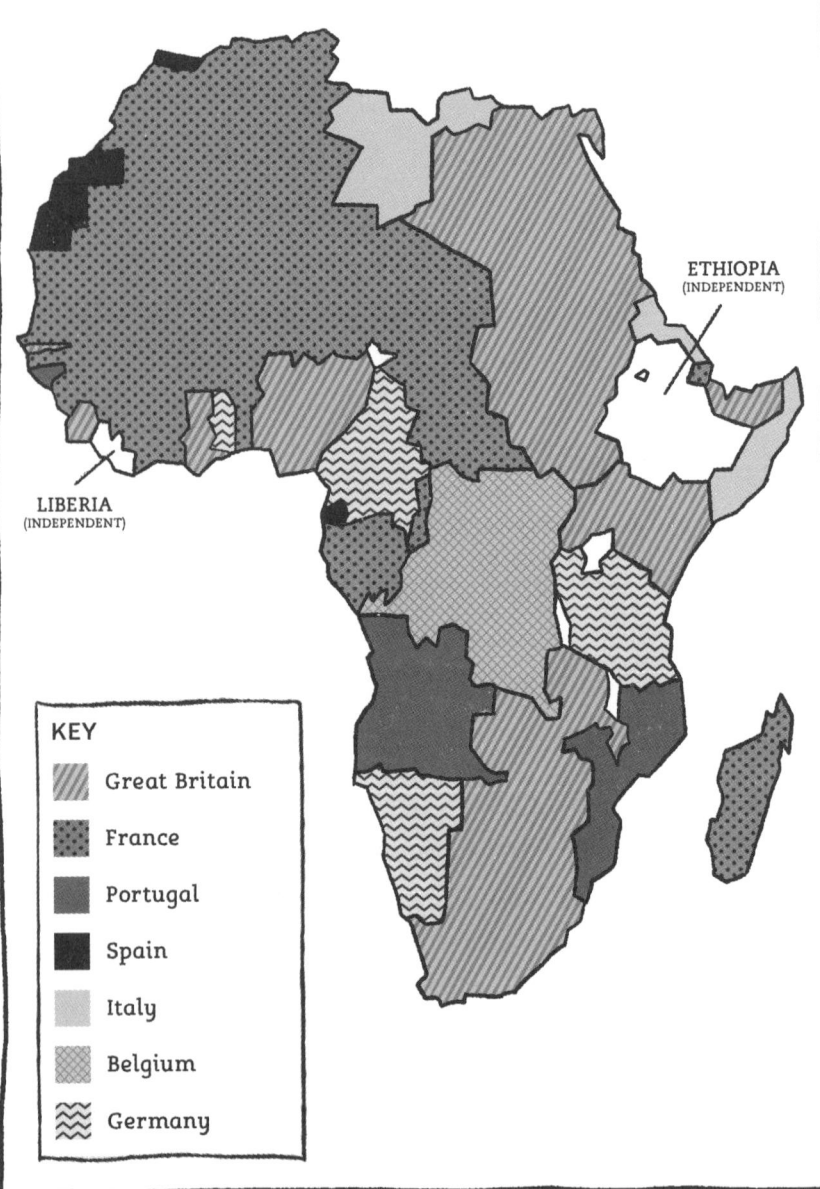

valuable goldmine. They failed but instead found thousands of tonnes of silver. It meant that Spain's empire was the richest in the world for a while.

The Spanish weren't the only ones conquering land around the world. The Dutch invaded much of what is now Indonesia and Malaysia. Sweden conquered most of the land surrounding the Baltic Sea. And the Ottoman army, marching from its home in the eastern Mediterranean, took vast areas of Europe and Asia as well as land in Africa.

And Africa was the valuable prize that so many of these countries most wanted. By the nineteenth century, seven different nations were competing with each other to conquer as much of it as they could. Great Britain, France, Germany, Belgium, Italy, Portugal and Spain all tried to expand their empires in what became known as the "Scramble for Africa".

Before this happened, Africa was mostly ruled by Africans like the Oba. The only areas of Africa where Europeans were in control were small forts and trading posts along the coast. This began to change as European explorers trekked further inland.

Then missionaries arrived, trying to persuade Africans to abandon their traditional gods and become Christians. The missionaries believed they were bringing civilisation to what Europeans called the "Dark Continent". In fact, they were helping to destroy many ancient beliefs and cultures.

The Scramble for Africa happened because many African countries were rich in the sorts of natural resources that Europeans wanted. These included useful raw materials such as cotton, timber, coal and rubber, along with more precious things like ivory, gold, emeralds and diamonds.

THE SCRAMBLE FOR AFRICA

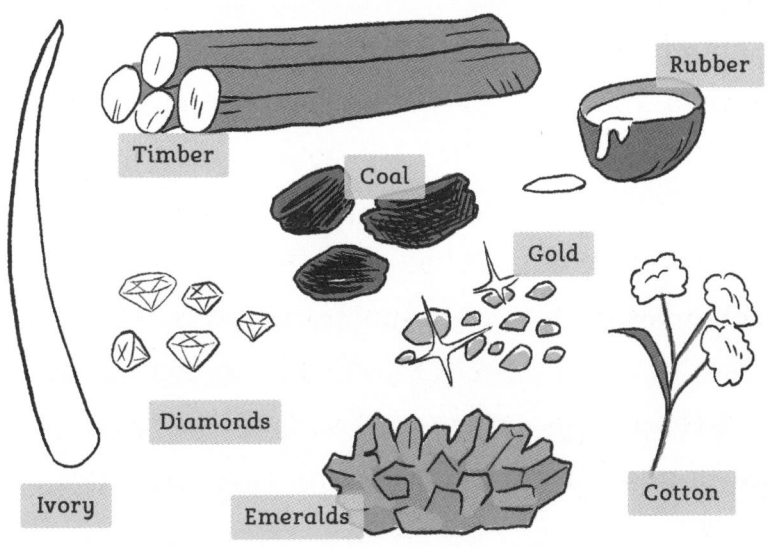

Unfortunately, these African countries were easy to attack. Their rulers were often weak or incompetent. They either had no army or one that was badly equipped compared to European armies.

The Kingdom of Benin was one of these vulnerable African countries. The Obas had been strong and successful for hundreds of years, but by the nineteenth century, their country had become one of those that couldn't defend itself against a European army. This was the result of several different problems.

For a long time, each new Oba had managed to control the most valuable trade that took place between the kingdom and any visitors. Usually, this meant keeping all the profits for himself instead of sharing it, and this caused a lot of bad feeling among his people.

The Oba's senior chieftains and advisers began to argue. Soon the country was almost torn apart by civil wars and by violent attempts to get rid of the ruler and put someone else on the throne. Many soldiers were killed or badly injured in these wars. This weakened the army so much that the Oba began to lose control. Neighbouring tribes that had once feared the Oba now started launching their own raids against his kingdom.

Benin's involvement in slavery was also problematic. Over hundreds of years, the trade in enslaved people had a devastating impact on this region. It destroyed the lives of the individual men and women who were enslaved and greatly reduced the local population. It is now believed that as many as 12 million people were taken out of Africa and shipped to colonies around the world. Few if any ever came back.

This terrible trade in lives was so profitable that many parts of Africa had become dependent on it. This all changed when the British decided to ban slavery in 1833. By this time, Britain was the most powerful nation on Earth and had the world's largest empire. Its ban threatened to disrupt the economy of the whole of the Slave Coast, especially when France introduced its own ban in 1848 and then America in 1865.

Britain still wanted to trade with Benin, but now it was mostly interested in woven cloth and natural resources such as rubber.

THE SCRAMBLE FOR AFRICA

The British also wanted to have more control over the trades it made with Benin. This upset Ovọnramwẹn, the new Oba, especially when he was asked to turn his country into something called a protectorate. This meant the Edo would give up their independence so that Benin could become part of the British Empire.

Ovọnramwẹn refused to do this and wouldn't sell anything except palm oil, which annoyed the British. In 1897, an Englishman called James Phillips travelled to Benin to meet with the Oba. He hoped that he could sort the problem out, but Ovọnramwẹn refused to see him because he was busy taking part in a large religious ceremony.

Phillips was determined to talk to the Oba anyway, and he and his men made their way towards the palace. They were attacked by a group of armed warriors, and several Britons were killed in the fighting, including Phillips. It is possible that the Edo thought the men had been on their way to kill the Oba, but there is no evidence for this.

The British authorities were furious when they heard about the deaths. Soon afterwards, they launched a military expedition to punish the Edo by getting rid of Ovọnramwẹn and taking over his kingdom.

The fighting was fierce, but it didn't last long. More than a thousand British troops stormed over the ancient defences of Benin City and then burned the palace to the ground.

It's not known how many people were killed on each side, but the Oba was ordered to leave the country as soon as the battle was over. After years of trying, Britain was finally in control of Benin.

9
LIFE IN NIGERIA

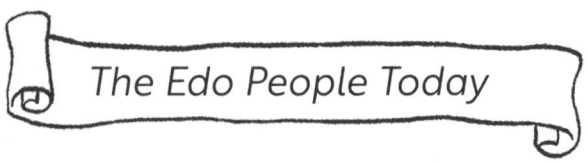
The Edo People Today

Thousands of items were stolen during the brutal destruction of Benin City, including its famous palace bronzes. Sadly, there is nothing unusual about this. Soldiers on the winning side often steal valuables from their enemies, but the theft of the Benin Bronzes is a very controversial subject.

This is partly because the Edo people still exist, and they want their bronzes back. Today, they live in a much larger country called Nigeria instead of having their own small kingdom, but their distinctive culture

has survived. The Edo still speak their own language, which is called Bini. They have an Oba, who is no longer the king but still an important figure to the Edo people. Many of the old traditions continue as well, and Edo children still play the sorts of games their ancestors played hundreds of years ago.

Most of the best Benin Bronzes are now in Europe and America. This includes museums in London and Berlin that have the largest collections of precious objects associated with Benin City and its ancient forest kingdom.

Politicians in Nigeria have asked for these items to be returned to West Africa, and the current Oba has made similar demands. Some Europeans and Americans also support these demands, but returning the bronzes is not straightforward.

Everyone agrees that the bronzes were stolen and that they shouldn't have been. It's also true that such items have a special connection to the places where they were created and that they form an important part of Nigeria's long history.

But there are people who believe the bronzes should stay where they are, in the great museums of London, Berlin and New York. They point out that these museums attract millions of visitors from around the world every year. By leaving the bronzes where they are, more people will see them than if they were sent back and put on display somewhere in Nigeria. As a result, this would help more of us to learn about different civilisations and the people who were part of them.

That sounds like a good thing, but it's a very complex problem when the objects involved are of great cultural and religious importance. More than a century after its destruction, Benin's spectacular artworks are the best clues we have to understanding this rich and extraordinary civilisation.

Our books are tested
for children and young people by
children and young people.

Thanks to everyone who consulted on
a manuscript for their time and effort in
helping us to make our books better
for our readers.